The Story Of WILLIAM PENN

Written and Illustrated by Aliki

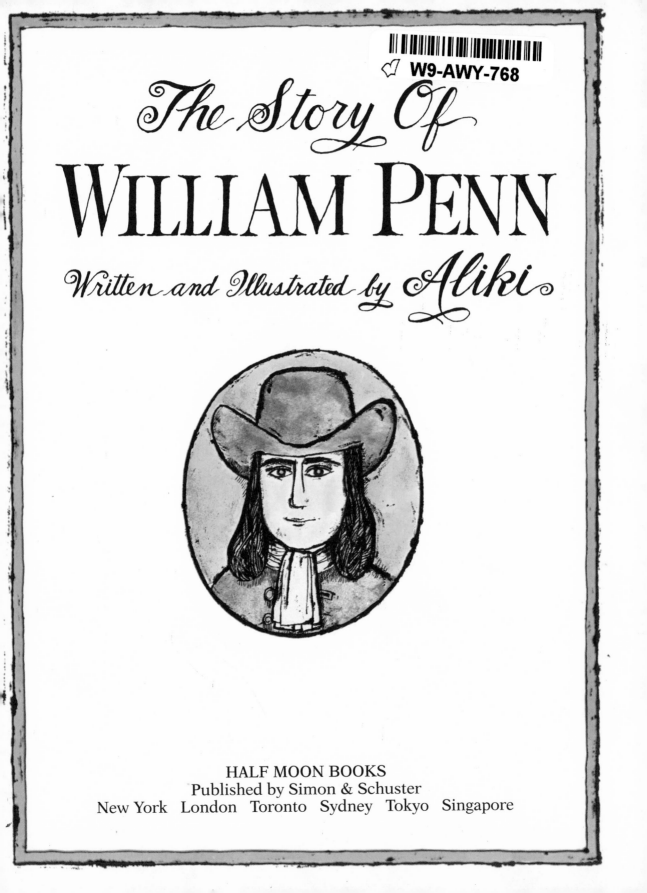

HALF MOON BOOKS
Published by Simon & Schuster
New York London Toronto Sydney Tokyo Singapore

HALF MOON BOOKS
Rockefeller Center
1230 Avenue of the Americas
New York, New York 10020
Copyright © 1964 by Aliki Brandenberg
Copyright renewed © 1992 by Aliki Brandenberg
First paperback edition 1994.
All rights reserved including the right of reproduction in whole or in part in any form.
HALF MOON BOOKS is a trademark of Simon & Schuster.
Also available in a SIMON & SCHUSTER BOOKS FOR YOUNG READERS hardcover edition.
The text for this book is set in New Aster.
The illustrations were done in water color and ink.
Manufactured in the United States of America.

10 9 8 7 6 5 4 3 2 1

Library of Congress Cataloging-in-Publication Data
Aliki. The story of William Penn/written and illustrated by Aliki. p. cm.
1. Penn, William, 1644-1718—Juvenile literature. 2. Pioneers—Pennsylvania—
Biography—Juvenile literature. 3. Quakers—Pennsylvania—Juvenile literature.
4. Pennsylvania—History—Colonial period, ca. 1600-1775—Juvenile literature.
[1. Penn, William, 1644-1718. 2. Quakers. 3. United States—History—Colonial
period, ca 1600-1775.] I. Title. F152.2.P4A44 1994 974.8'02'092—dc20 [B]
93-26289 CIP 0-671-88646-0 (PBK) 0-671-88558-8 (HC)

For

Dean
Jamie
Maria Nicole

and

all the other children of

Philadelphia

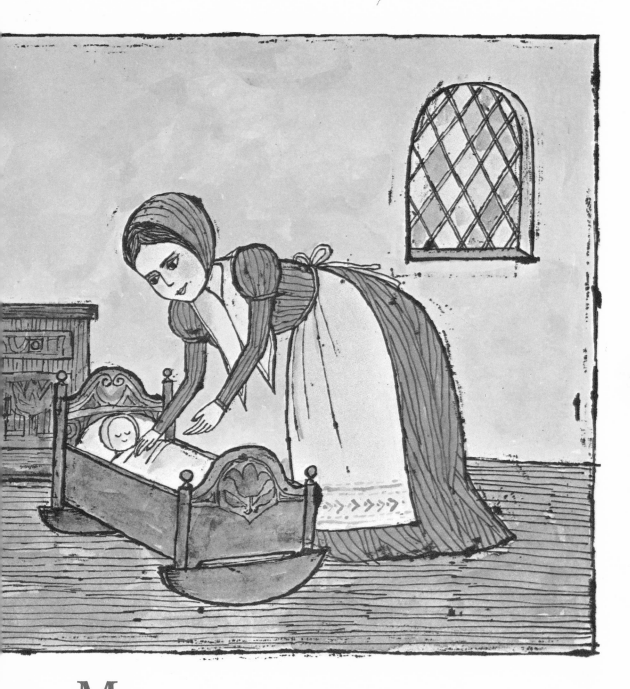

Many years ago there lived a man all the world
grew to know. His name was William Penn.

William lived in England with his wife and children,
whom he dearly loved.

William's kindness and wisdom won him many
friends. Some of them were ordinary people.
Some were noble. One was the king of England
himself, Charles II.

Although William was wealthy, he did not choose the
frivolous life of the rich. He wore no frills as they did.
He was a simple man who admired others for their
good deeds and not for what they owned.

William was a Quaker. The Quakers are gentle, peaceful people. They do not believe in fighting. They think that all people should live together in harmony.

But in those days, in England, people were not free
to say what they chose. They had to speak carefully,
or they were punished. Those who did not obey were
sent to prison.

William Penn was not afraid. He spoke to the people and told them to believe as they wished. He wrote books and traveled to other countries, telling everyone about freedom.

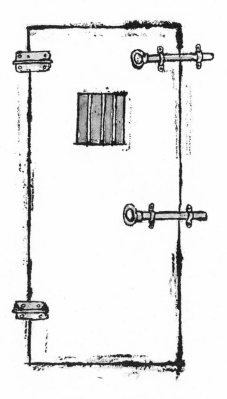

William, too, was sent to prison for a while because he spoke so freely. Yet he never lost hope that all men and women could live together in harmony.

As the years passed, more and more people grew to know and respect William Penn and to believe in his ideas.

Now King Charles happened to owe William a huge sum of money. When the king finally paid his debt, he gave William a large piece of land in America instead of the money.

William had heard of the New World, and of those who went there to seek a better life. He had long dreamed of going there himself.

William set to work, finding others to go with him. He told them that in America they would be free to think and speak as they pleased.

William called his new land Pennsylvania—the woods of Penn.

He planned where a city would be built, and he named the city Philadelphia—the city of brotherly love.

When everything was ready, William bid his family
farewell, for they would join him later. The sails were
spread and the brave group left their homeland.

The journey was long. The ship moved slowly onward, rocking and tossing on the white-capped waves. Many people fell ill, and everyone wanted the voyage to end.

Two long months passed.

Then one day in 1682 they saw their new land. They saw wigwams nestled among the trees and Native Americans watching them from a distance.

And on the shore stood some earlier settlers, who had come from afar to welcome them.

And they rejoiced.

But the Native Americans, who were called Indians, were uneasy. Many of their people had been chased from their land and hurt by other settlers.

William wanted to make friends with the Native Americans. He did not want them to be afraid of him and of his people, so he invited them to a meeting.

The Indians came, wearing their finest headdresses. Both settlers and natives gave each other gifts in the shade of an old elm tree.

William Penn wrote a Peace Treaty that said:
In this land our two peoples will live
together in respect and freedom.

He proved to all the world that people can live in harmony if they choose.

The Native Americans trusted William because he was fair. He did not chase them from their land but bought it from them.

He visited their homes and respected their customs. He even learned to speak their language and said it was the most beautiful language of all.

William's city grew. More houses were built, and
new settlers came in great numbers.

To this day, the father of Philadelphia looks down over his people. And his people look up to him with pride.

STEP INTO READING® will help your child get there. The program offers five steps to reading success. Each step includes fun stories and colorful art or photographs. In addition to original fiction and books with favorite characters, there are Step into Reading Non-Fiction Readers, Phonics Readers and Boxed Sets, Sticker Readers, and Comic Readers—a complete literacy program with something to interest every child.

Learning to Read, Step by Step!

Ready to Read   Preschool–Kindergarten
• big type and easy words • rhyme and rhythm • picture clues
For children who know the alphabet and are eager to begin reading.

Reading with Help   Preschool–Grade 1
• basic vocabulary • short sentences • simple stories
For children who recognize familiar words and sound out new words with help.

Reading on Your Own   Grades 1–3
• engaging characters • easy-to-follow plots • popular topics
For children who are ready to read on their own.

Reading Paragraphs   Grades 2–3
• challenging vocabulary • short paragraphs • exciting stories
For newly independent readers who read simple sentences with confidence.

Ready for Chapters   Grades 2–4
• chapters • longer paragraphs • full-color art
For children who want to take the plunge into chapter books but still like colorful pictures.

STEP INTO READING® is designed to give every child a successful reading experience. The grade levels are only guides; children will progress through the steps at their own speed, developing confidence in their reading.

Remember, a lifetime love of reading starts with a single step!

RHUS39292

All rights reserved. Published in the United States by Random House Children's Books, a division of Penguin Random House LLC, 1745 Broadway, New York, NY 10019, and in Canada by Penguin Random House Canada Limited, Toronto.

Step into Reading, Random House, and the Random House colophon are registered trademarks of Penguin Random House LLC.

Visit us on the Web!
StepIntoReading.com
randomhousekids.com

Educators and librarians, for a variety of teaching tools, visit us at RHTeachersLibrarians.com

ISBN 978-1-5247-7037-2 (trade) — ISBN 978-1-5247-7038-9 (lib. bdg.)
ISBN 978-1-5247-7039-6 (ebook)

Printed in the United States of America

10 9 8 7 6 5 4 3 2 1

A Colorful Christmas!

by Xiomara Nieves

Random House 🏠 New York

Frosty the Snowman
loves all the colors
at Christmas!

There is white,
fluffy snow.

There is a black

magic hat.

Frosty wears
a long red scarf.

Musicians in blue
uniforms play
instruments.

There are presents tied
with purple ribbons.

A man sells green
Christmas trees.

The woodland animals
put orange ornaments
on a tree.

There is a yellow star
on top of
a Christmas tree.

Frosty shares a pink
treat with his friends.

Here comes jolly
Santa Claus
with his reindeer.

Santa wears a red suit,
and his reindeer
are brown.
His sleigh is filled
with colorful gifts.

There is a purple ball.

There is a blue train.

There is a brown
teddy bear.

There is a green robot.

Have a colorful
Christmas!

Dear Parents:

Congratulations! Your child is taking the first steps on an exciting journey. The destination? Independent reading!

STEP INTO READING® will help your child get there. The program offers five steps to reading success. Each step includes fun stories and colorful art or photographs. In addition to original fiction and books with favorite characters, there are Step into Reading Non-Fiction Readers, Phonics Readers and Boxed Sets, Sticker Readers, and Comic Readers—a complete literacy program with something to interest every child.

Learning to Read, Step by Step!

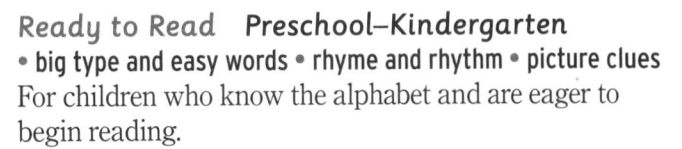

Ready to Read   Preschool–Kindergarten
• big type and easy words • rhyme and rhythm • picture clues
For children who know the alphabet and are eager to begin reading.

Reading with Help   Preschool–Grade 1
• basic vocabulary • short sentences • simple stories
For children who recognize familiar words and sound out new words with help.

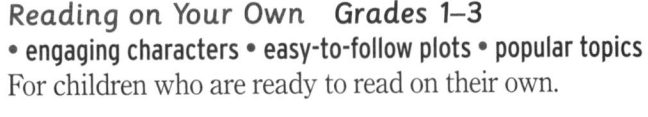

Reading on Your Own   Grades 1–3
• engaging characters • easy-to-follow plots • popular topics
For children who are ready to read on their own.

Reading Paragraphs   Grades 2–3
• challenging vocabulary • short paragraphs • exciting stories
For newly independent readers who read simple sentences with confidence.

Ready for Chapters   Grades 2–4
• chapters • longer paragraphs • full-color art
For children who want to take the plunge into chapter books but still like colorful pictures.

STEP INTO READING® is designed to give every child a successful reading experience. The grade levels are only guides; children will progress through the steps at their own speed, developing confidence in their reading.

Remember, a lifetime love of reading starts with a single step!

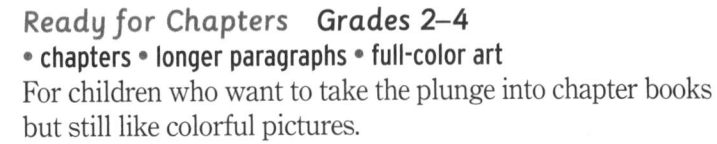

For Matt, my big little brother –C.B.C.

RHUS39292

All rights reserved. Published in the United States by Random House Children's Books, a division of Penguin Random House LLC, 1745 Broadway, New York, NY 10019, and in Canada by Penguin Random House Canada Limited, Toronto.

Step into Reading, Random House, and the Random House colophon are registered trademarks of Penguin Random House LLC.

Visit us on the Web!
StepIntoReading.com
randomhousekids.com

Educators and librarians, for a variety of teaching tools, visit us at RHTeachersLibrarians.com

ISBN 978-1-5247-7037-2 (trade) — ISBN 978-1-5247-7038-9 (lib. bdg.)
ISBN 978-1-5247-7039-6 (ebook)

Printed in the United States of America

10 9 8 7 6 5 4 3 2 1

FROSTY the SNOWMAN™

SNOW DAY!

adapted by Courtney B. Carbone

illustrated by Fabio Laguna and Andrea Cagol

Random House 🏠 New York

A magician named
Professor Hinkle
came to school.
He had a funny bunny.

Professor Hinkle's tricks
did not work!
He threw away
his magic hat.

The school bell rang.

The kids ran outside.

They made a snowman
and named him Frosty!

He had a corncob pipe,
a button nose,
and two eyes
made out of coal.

A gust of winter wind
blew the magician's hat
through the air.
It landed on Frosty.

Frosty came to life!
"Happy birthday!"
he said with a smile.
The kids cheered.

Professor Hinkle took
his magic hat back!

The bunny

returned the hat

to Frosty.

He came back to life!

Frosty was so much fun.

He danced and sang.

He led a parade

through town!

Suddenly, Frosty
began to melt!
He had to go
someplace cold.

A girl named Karen
found a train going north.

The train car was
great for Frosty.
But it was too cold
for Karen.

They got off the train
at the next stop.
Professor Hinkle had
followed them.

Frosty and Karen
needed to escape.
Frosty raced down a hill
with Karen on his back.

They went inside
a greenhouse,
where it was warm.
The magician found them.
He locked them inside!

"Oh, no!" Karen cried.

Frosty melted

into a puddle of water.

The bunny went
to get help.
Santa Claus came
to the rescue!

Santa unlocked the door.
A winter wind blew in
and froze the water.
Frosty came back
to life!

"Happy birthday!"

he said again.

Karen was so happy!

Santa took Karen home.
Frosty would go
to the North Pole
with Santa!

Frosty promised

to come back and visit.

Now every year,
Frosty returns with
the magical snow!
Happy holidays!